WALT DISNEY
Dumbo

Twin Books

Early one morning, while most people were still fast asleep, a flock of storks appeared in the sky. They had been flying all night and were very happy to catch a glimpse of a large tent surrounded by a group of smaller tents and trailers.

"There, below! It's the circus!" shouted one of the storks as he released his bundle. Soon all the other storks let go of their parcels, and the sky was filled with parachutes carrying blue and pink bundles. A gentle breeze delivered the drifting arrivals right to the tents.

Mrs. Giraffe, the tallest, was the first to spot the bundles. "Wake up, everyone! The storks have come," she called. "Our little ones are here!"

Baby giraffes, tigers, hippopotami, bears and kangaroos floated down to their waiting mothers. The animals ran this way and that to catch their young. The baby tiger landed gently next to his mother, and the baby giraffe reached out her long neck and licked her mother on the way down.

Mrs. Jumbo, the elephant, watched as each baby arrived. Even after the sky was empty, she continued to look up.

"Oh, dear," she sighed. "I was certain there would be a bundle for me. Now I'll have to wait until next year." She began to cry.

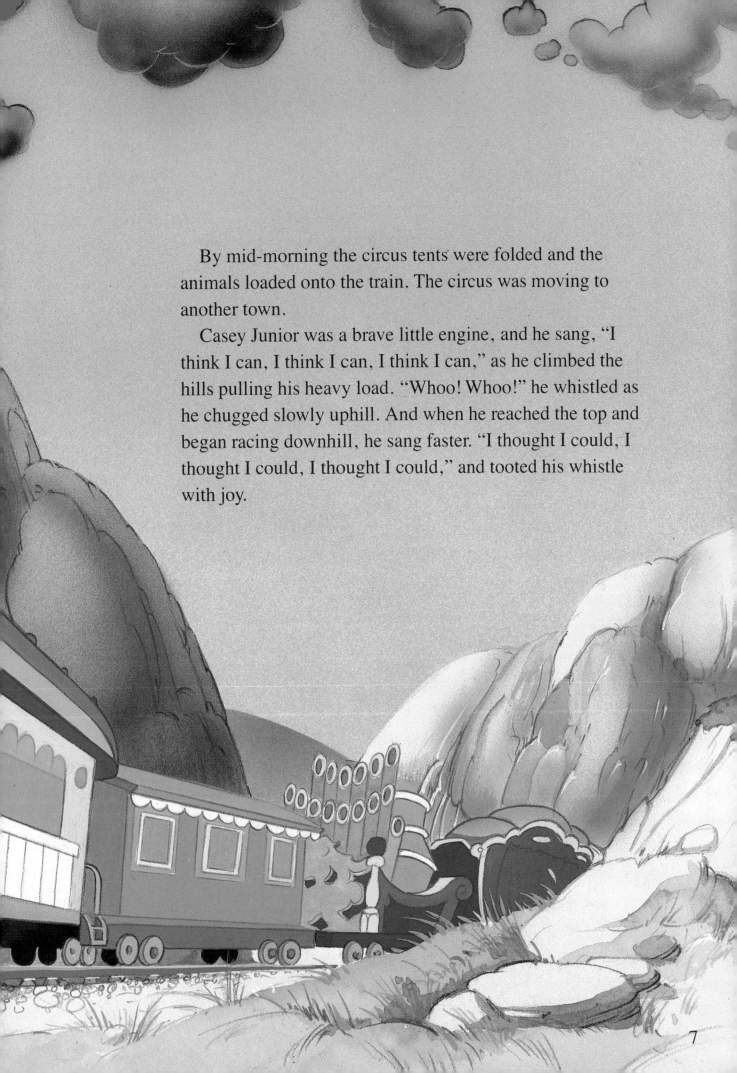

By mid-morning the circus tents were folded and the animals loaded onto the train. The circus was moving to another town.

Casey Junior was a brave little engine, and he sang, "I think I can, I think I can, I think I can," as he climbed the hills pulling his heavy load. "Whoo! Whoo!" he whistled as he chugged slowly uphill. And when he reached the top and began racing downhill, he sang faster. "I thought I could, I thought I could, I thought I could," and tooted his whistle with joy.

As the train sped along the tracks, a small shape moved along the tops of the cars. It was a stork, carrying a large bundle and shouting, "Mrs. Jumbo! Special delivery for Mrs. Jumbo!"

Hearing the stork's shouts, two of the elephants stuck their trunks through an opening and waved. "Over here," they signalled.

9

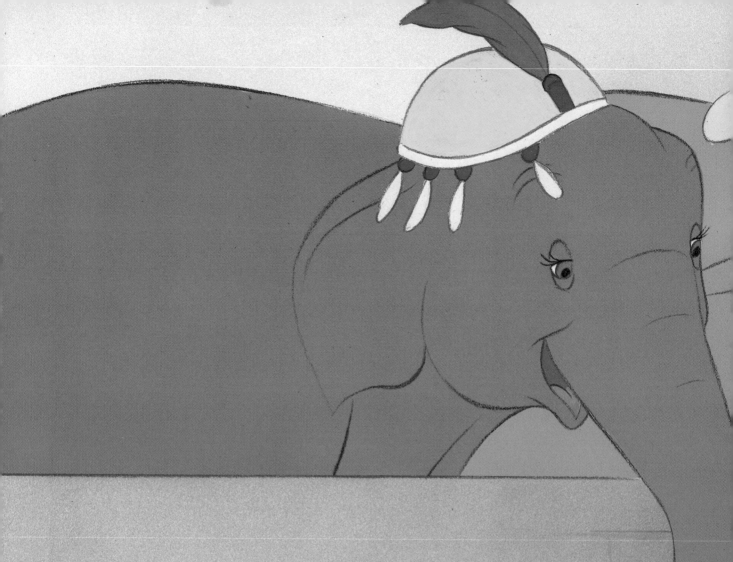

The stork lowered his heavy bundle into the wagon.

"Better late than never," he said, tipping his cap.

"You'd better check to make sure he's yours," he said, as Mrs. Jumbo untied the parcel.

"He looks perfect!" exclaimed Mrs. Jumbo, staring proudly at her new baby. His duty done, the stork bowed to Mrs. Jumbo and was on his way. The other elephants crowded around the new arrival.

"Isn't he just adorable?" one of them cooed.

"Looks just like his mother," said another, and the other elephants nodded their heads in agreement.

All this attention was too much for the little elephant. Letting out a big sneeze, he shook his head, exposing two enormous floppy ears.

"Take a look at those ears," said one of the elephants, stretching one of his ears with her trunk.

"Too bad the stork has already left," sniggered another. "You should file a complaint." The elephants all began to laugh.

"I never saw anything so dumb-looking in all my life. We'll have to call him Dumbo," said the biggest elephant, causing more laughter.

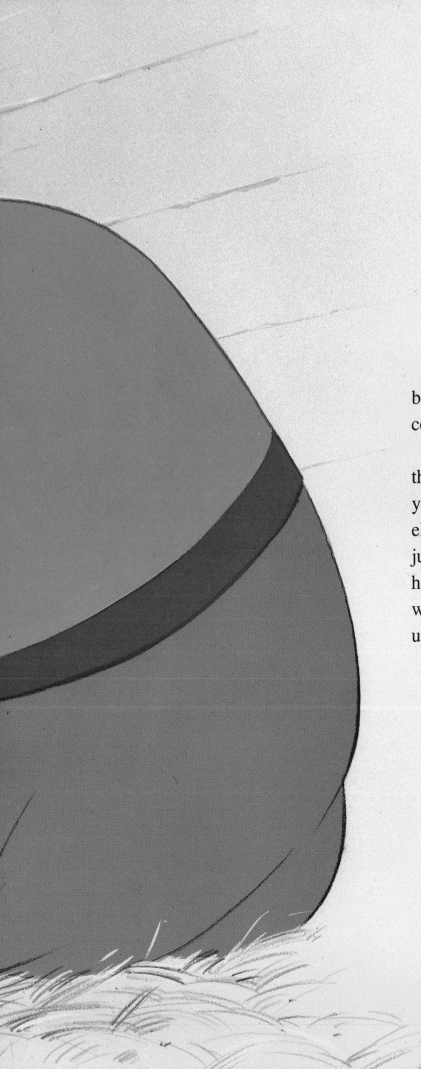

Mrs. Jumbo picked up her baby and stormed off to a corner so they could be alone.

"Don't pay any attention to them," she said softly. "I think you are the most handsome elephant in the world. They're just jealous." And she cuddled him and gently stroked his head with her trunk. Dumbo smiled up at her.

Late that night the train finally reached the town where the circus was to perform. The animals were unloaded and the tents were pitched.

The next morning a parade was held to announce the circus's arrival. Proud camels led the way, followed by the ringmaster, who shouted to the crowd: "Ladies and gentlemen! Boys and girls! Come to the Big Top tonight! We'll make you laugh! We'll make you cry! We'll thrill you with wonderful acts you've never seen before! All this and more at the circus!"

Behind the ringmaster, the hippo yawned as he hauled the 33-ton pipe organ along.

An endless stream of animals passed through the town. Kangaroos carried their babies in their pouches and hopped along beside bears, while lions roared from their cages, frightening the crowd.

Bringing up the rear were the elephants, and last of all was little Dumbo. Clutching his mother's tail, Dumbo looked around in wonder. This was his first parade, and it was all very exciting. He dreamed of the day when he would be at the head of the procession.

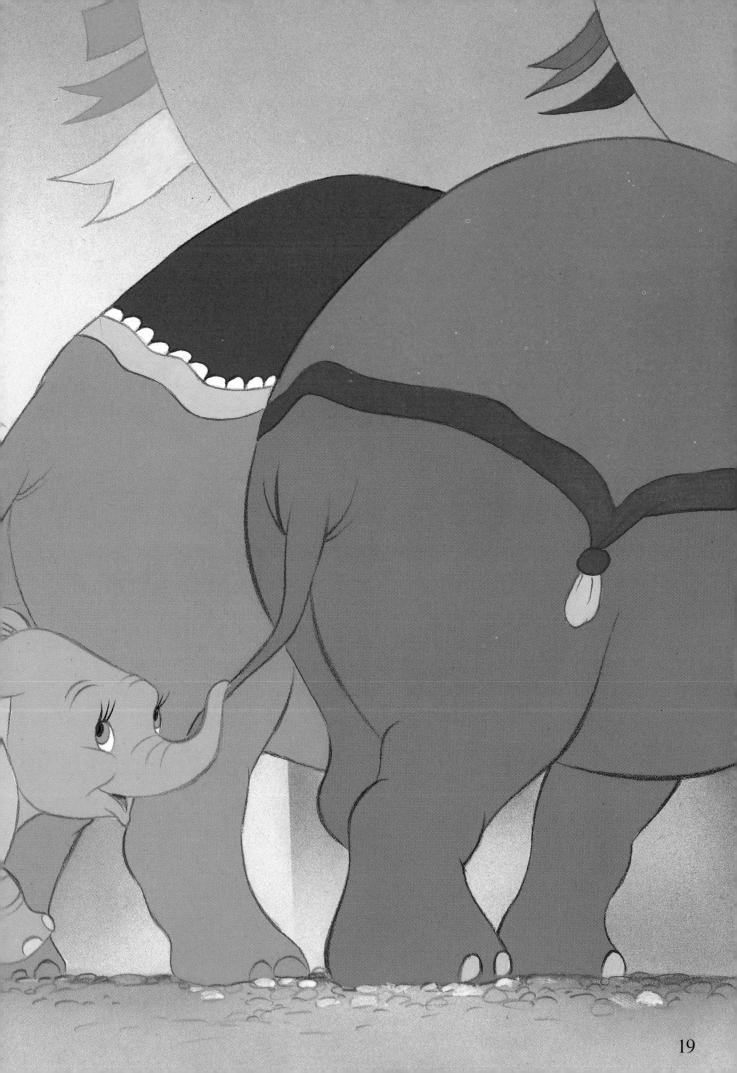

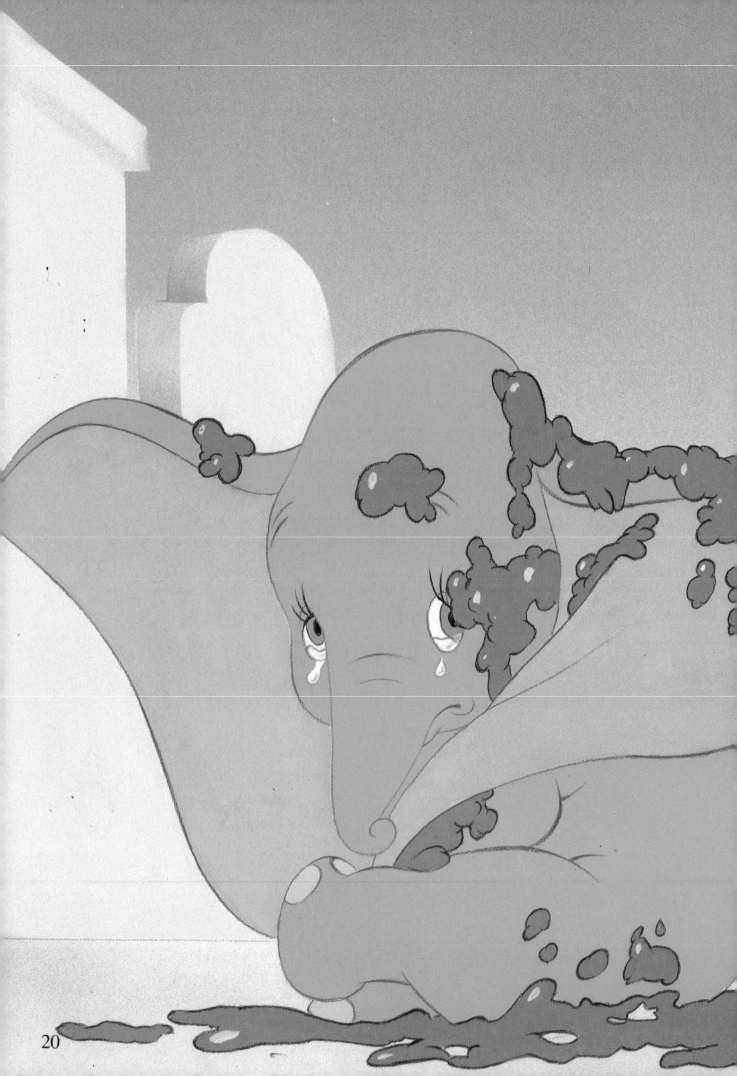

Lost in his daydreams, Dumbo didn't look where he was going. He stepped on one of his enormous ears and tumbled headfirst into a mud puddle. Seeing the little elephant trip made the crowd laugh.

"Look at those ears!" a boy shouted. "They'd make the biggest slingshot in the world." He reached over and pulled at one of Dumbo's ears. It snapped back and knocked the little elephant over again. The crowd laughed and jeered even more.

Dumbo was filled with shame. Tears fell as he unsuccessfully tried to wrap himself up in his huge ears.

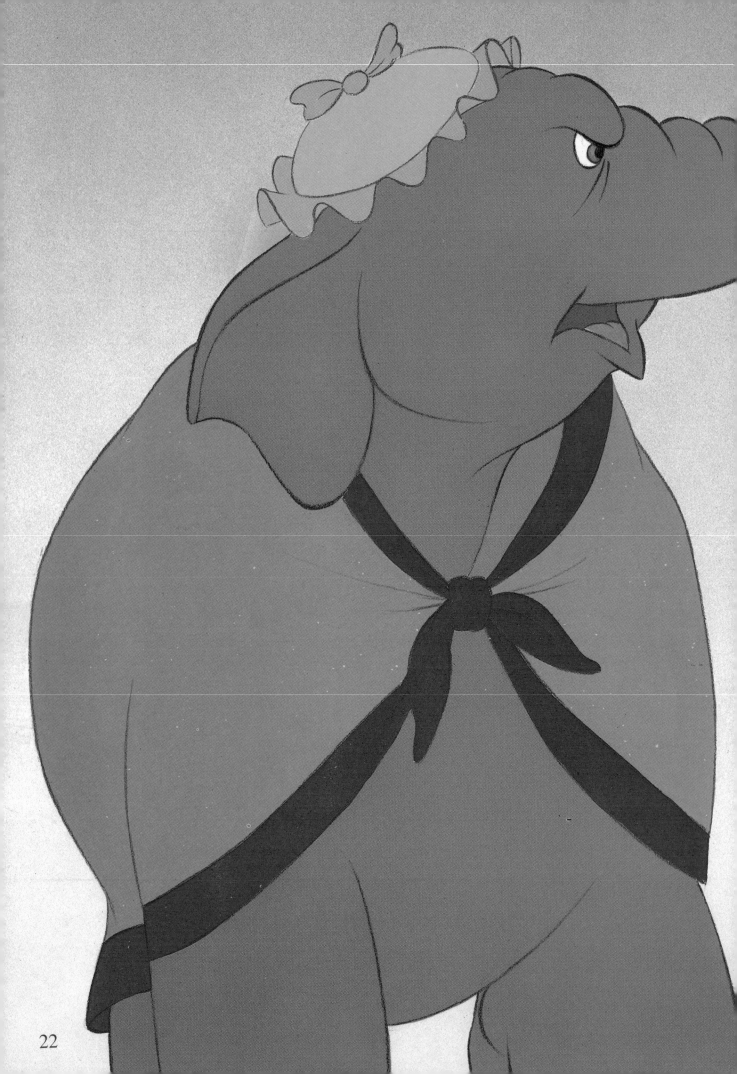

22

The boy reached out and pulled one of his ears again. This time Dumbo cried out in pain. Hearing her baby cry, Mrs. Jumbo rushed to his aid, trumpeting in anger. She grabbed the boy with her trunk and lifted him into the air. The boy was frightened and began to yell.

"Help! Help!" he shouted. "You're hurting me." Which, of course, was not true. Mrs. Jumbo only wanted to teach him a lesson, and so she placed him gently back on the ground.

But the crowd had become hysterical. Thinking that Mrs. Jumbo was wild, they called for help. "That elephant is crazy! Do something! She's dangerous!" shouted the bystanders.

The trainers came running with ropes, which they threw around Mrs. Jumbo's neck.

Mrs. Jumbo reared up on her hind legs and shrieked in protest, but it was too late. The ropes tightened around her and she was led away. "Lock her up!" shouted the ringmaster.

Poor little Dumbo looked after his mother as she was led away. Now he was all alone.

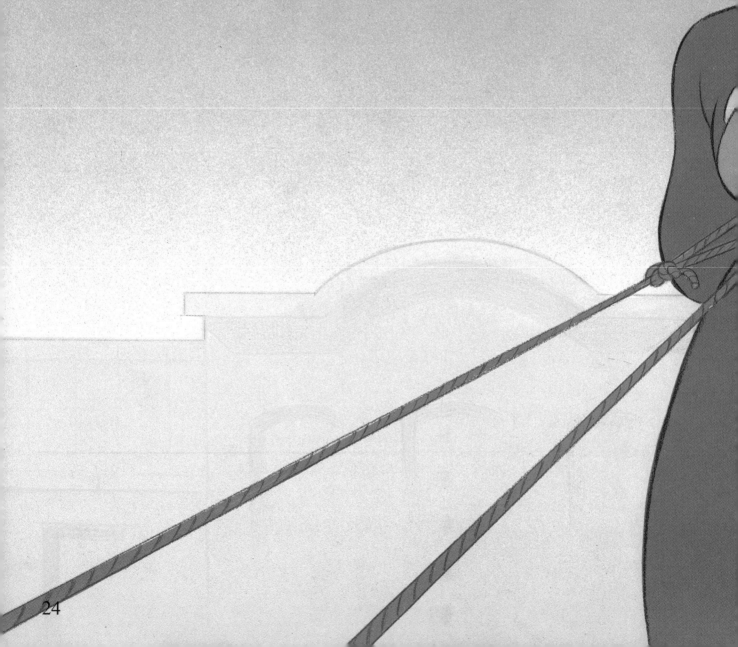

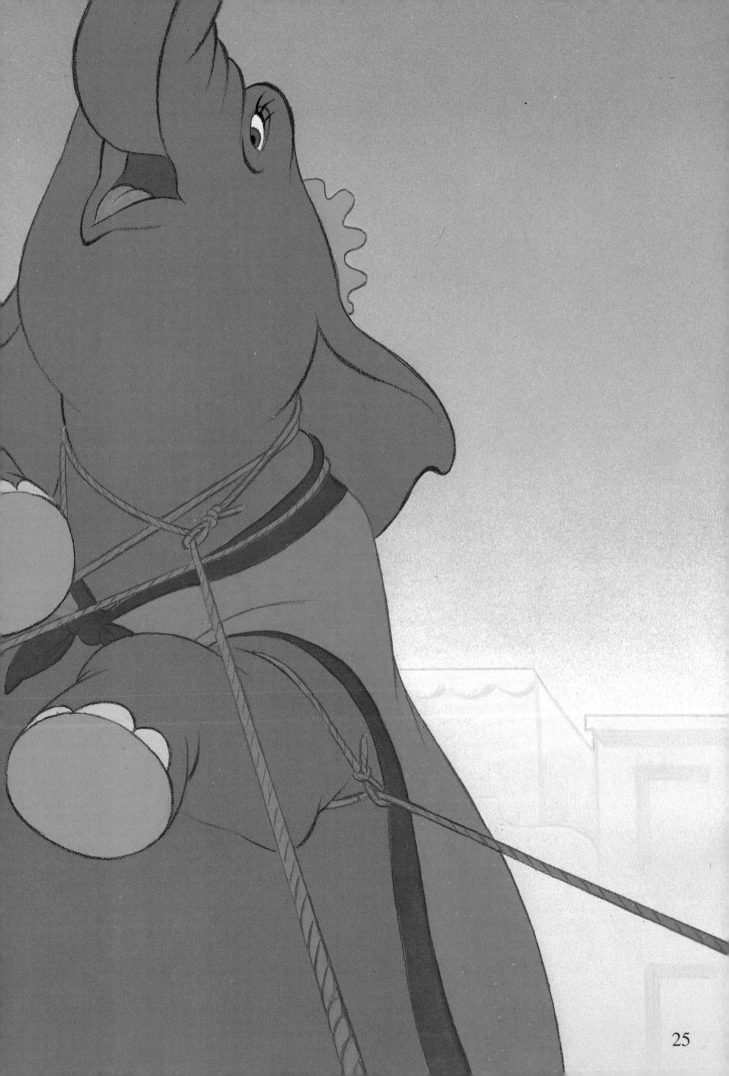

He looked for the other elephants, hoping to find out where his mother was. But when the elephants saw Dumbo coming, they turned their backs on him.

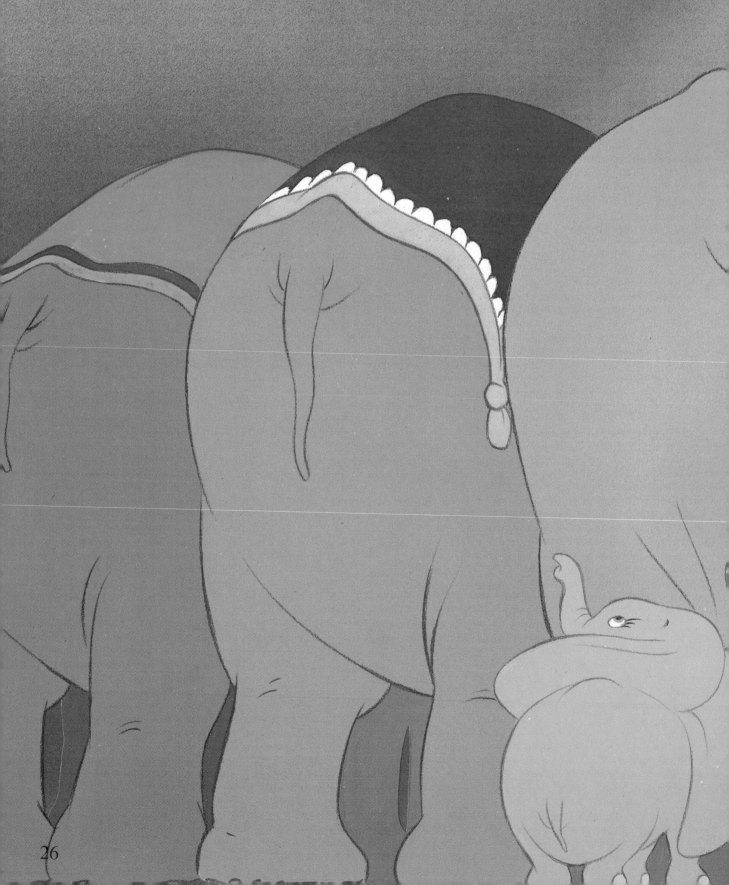

"What a disgrace. All that fuss for a floppy-eared little runt," said one of the elephants.

"Nothing would have happened if it weren't for that Dumbo! It's all his fault," replied another.

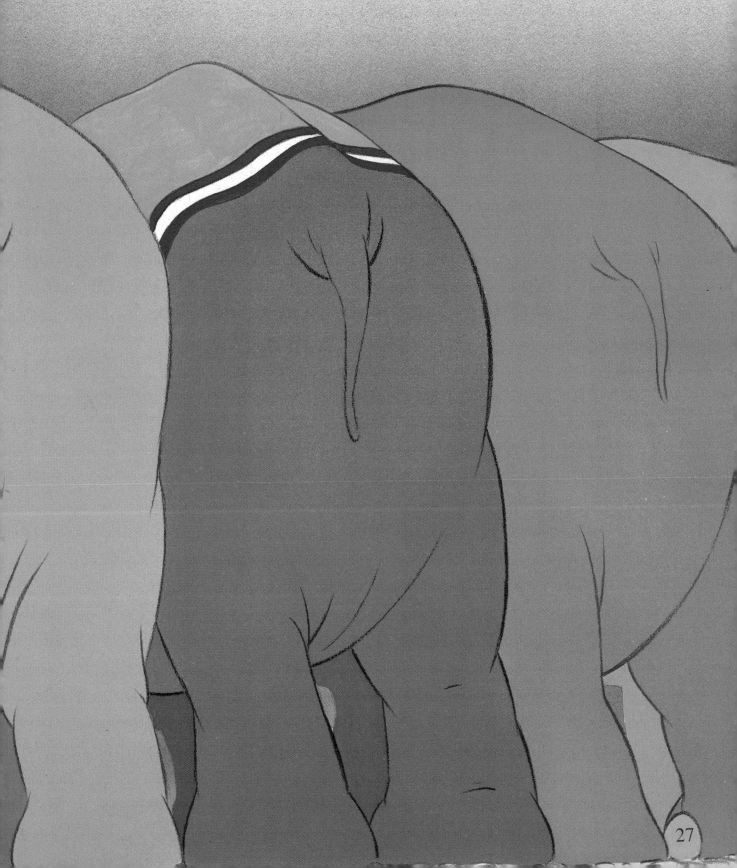

Poor Dumbo sat down and began to cry. As he sobbed
quietly in the corner, he felt something tickling his trunk. It
was a little mouse.

"Don't be sad, Dumbo. I'm your friend," whispered the
mouse. "I heard what they said about you and I'm going to
teach those gossiping pachyderms a lesson."

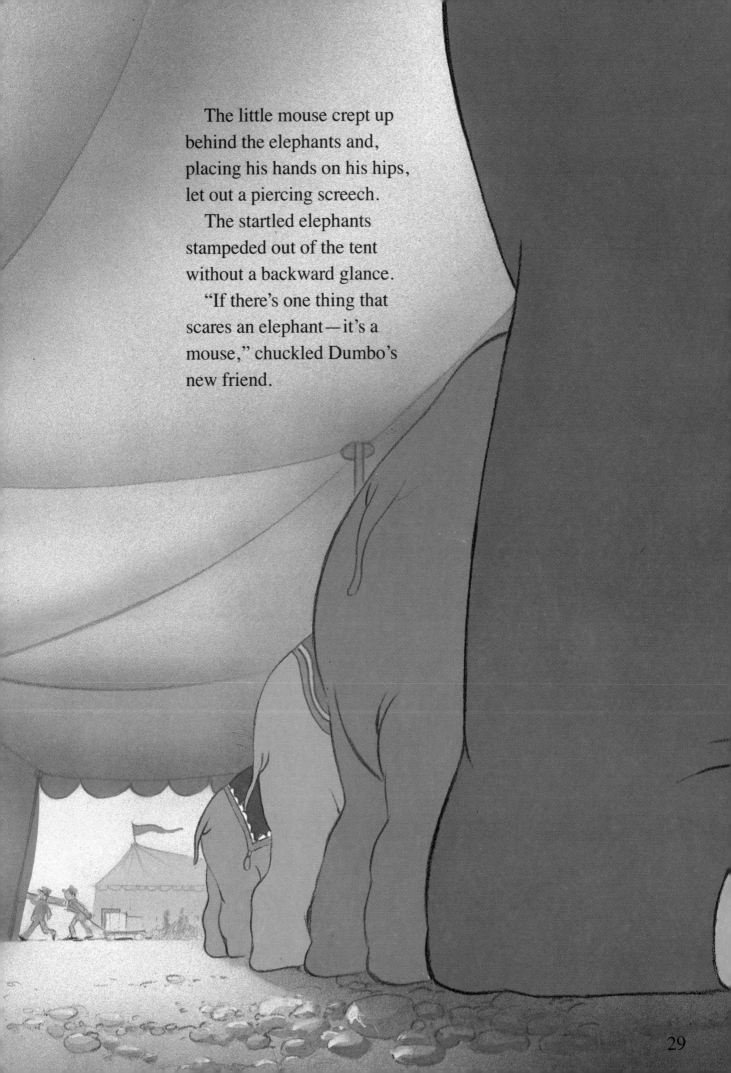

The little mouse crept up
behind the elephants and,
placing his hands on his hips,
let out a piercing screech.

The startled elephants
stampeded out of the tent
without a backward glance.

"If there's one thing that
scares an elephant—it's a
mouse," chuckled Dumbo's
new friend.

Dumbo looked at the little mouse with admiration. The mouse bowed. "Timothy's the name," he said. "I may be small, but don't let my size fool you. I get around, and no one notices me. I know everything that goes on in this circus. I know that your mother's been locked away, and I also know that you're ashamed of your ears. Well, I think they're great. Those ears are going to make you famous one of these days. Stick with me, kid. I've got big plans for you."

And so Dumbo found a friend in the form of a spunky little mouse.

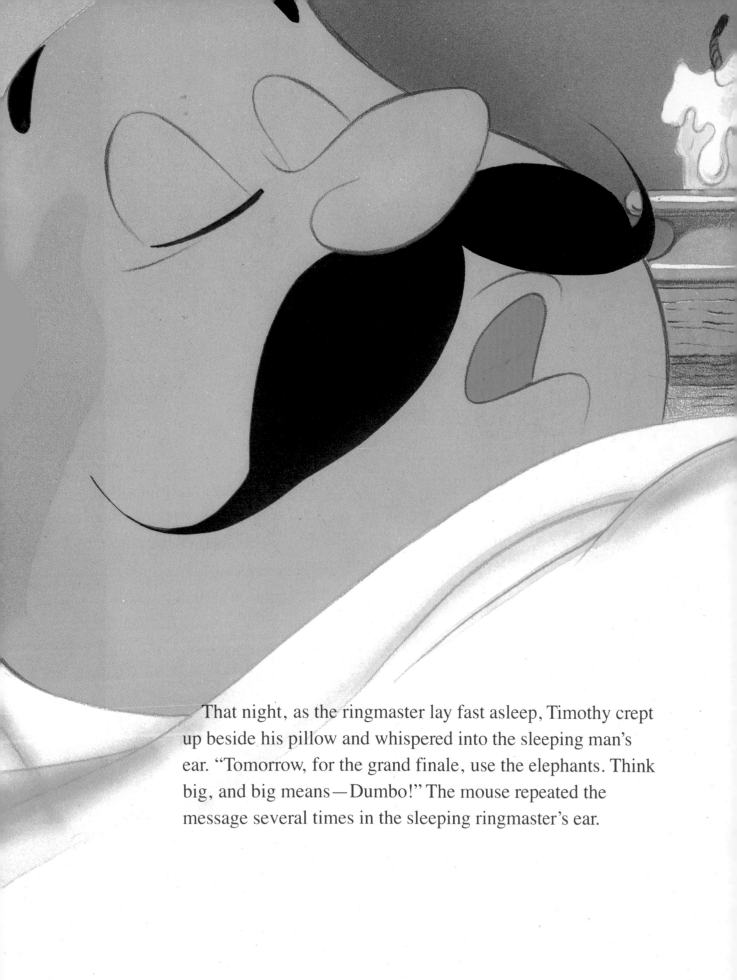

That night, as the ringmaster lay fast asleep, Timothy crept
up beside his pillow and whispered into the sleeping man's
ear. "Tomorrow, for the grand finale, use the elephants. Think
big, and big means—Dumbo!" The mouse repeated the
message several times in the sleeping ringmaster's ear.

The next morning the ringmaster awoke with a smile on his face. "I've got a wonderful idea for the new grand finale," he said. "I'll use the elephants and that little Dumbo, too. And to think that I thought of it all by myself." With that, he rushed off to prepare the new act.

That night, standing under the spotlight, surrounded by elephants balancing on their hind legs, the ringmaster announced the grand finale.

"Ladies and gentlemen! We will now present for your entertainment the most stupendous, magnificent, super-colossal spectacle ever witnessed!" shouted the ringmaster. As the audience held its breath, an elephant climbed onto a large ball. The crowd watched in amazement as elephant after elephant climbed on top of each other, forming a pyramid.

"Ouch! Take your foot out of my eye," grumbled the elephant on the bottom.

"Gaining a little weight, aren't you?" mumbled another elephant, sagging under the weight of her friend.

"And now for the grand finale," shouted the ringmaster. "Little Dumbo will leap from a springboard onto the top of this pyramid of pachyderms." The ringmaster signalled for a drumroll.

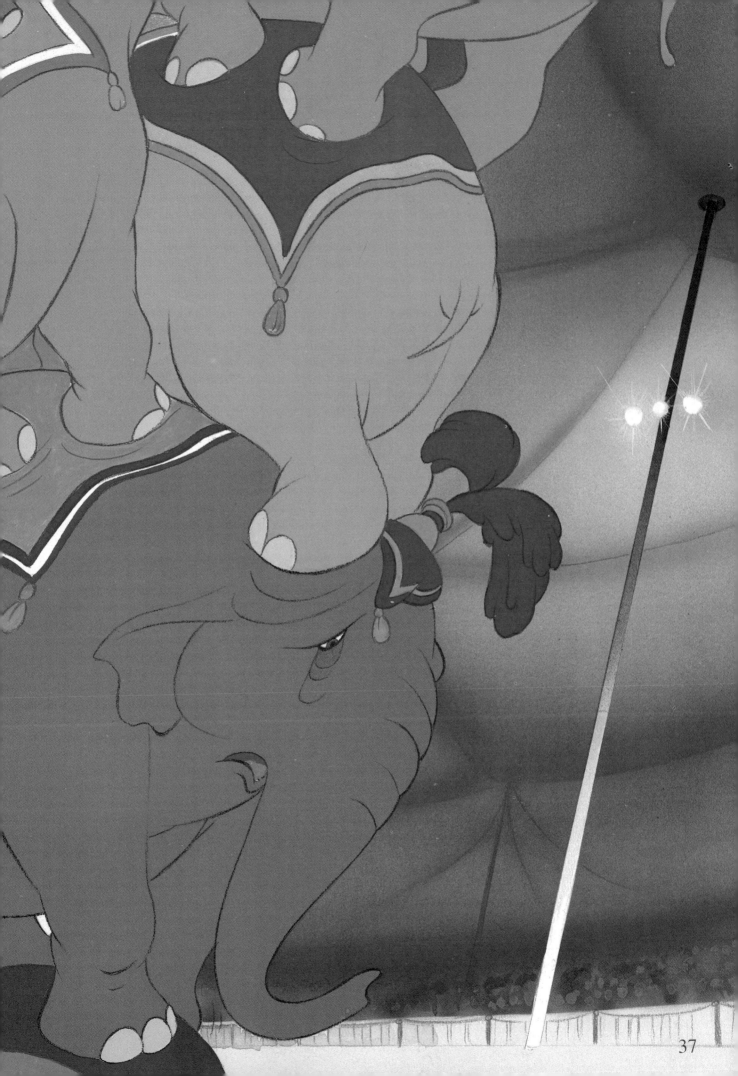

The bright spotlight shone down on the opening of a little tent, where Dumbo stood frozen with stage fright. Timothy the mouse had tied the little elephant's ears out of the way. He gave Dumbo a nudge and whispered, "Go ahead, kid. Show them what you're made of."

Dumbo gathered his courage and began to run into the big ring toward the springboard. As he ran, his ears came untied and flopped down. The audience gasped as Dumbo tripped and went flying, head over heels, bumping right into the ball on which the elephants were balanced.

For a split second all was silent. Then a faint creaking was heard as the elephants began to sway back and forth. The people in the audience ran for their lives, as the huge pyramid of elephants began to collapse.

One of the falling elephants landed on the trapeze, and another clung to her tail. Back and forth they went. "I can't hold on much longer," shouted the elephant who was holding on by her trunk.

The ringmaster stood by helplessly. There was nothing he could do.

Finally, giving a loud cry, the elephant on the trapeze fell, taking her friend with her. As if blown by a strong wind, the circus tent began to billow. Then it collapsed.

Fortunately, except for a few bumps and bruises, no one had been badly hurt. Dumbo, however, was in serious trouble.

"A star! Huh!" snorted the ringmaster. "You're nothing but a bumbling, bungling clown. So that's exactly what you can be."

Dumbo's face was painted and he was forced to stand in the ring waving a little flag. Night after night Dumbo played the fool as clowns threw cream pies in his face and audiences laughed and jeered.

One day the clowns came up with a new act for Dumbo. They built a large house and made believe it was on fire. At the very top was Dumbo, wearing a baby bonnet.

Dressed as firemen, the clowns ran around frantically, waving fire hoses and squirting everything. One clown held up a tiny ladder. "Do you think this is long enough?" he asked, as the audience roared with laughter.

"That ladder is much too short," shouted one of the clowns. "The baby will have to jump!"

"Jump, baby! We'll catch you," yelled the firemen, who were holding a safety net.

Dumbo looked down, shaking with fright. It was a long way down, and the net didn't look very strong. The fumes from the make-believe fire hurt his eyes. The audience began to chant, "Jump! Jump!"

Dumbo closed his eyes and leaped into the air. His ears flapped out behind him.

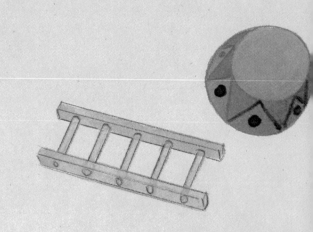

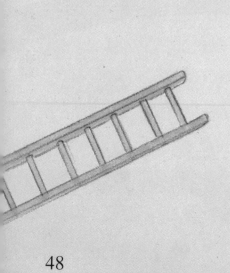

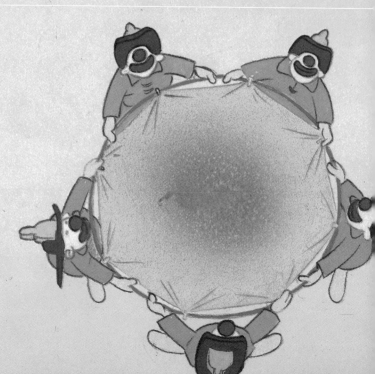

Dumbo opened his eyes and saw the net below him. But his ordeal wasn't over. The net tore under his weight, and Dumbo fell into a tub of water, making a big splash.

The audience roared with laughter at the sight of the big, wet baby. Soon the laughter turned into applause, but the clowns were the ones who took the bows. Ashamed and still shaking, Dumbo walked sadly out of the circus tent. He had never felt so miserable in his life.

Timothy found Dumbo shivering in a corner.

"What you need is a good rubdown, and you'll feel better in no time," said Timothy, taking up a sponge and scrubbing off the make-up. "Cheer up, Dumbo! I've got some good news for you. I've found out where they're keeping your mother. Tonight at midnight, I'll take you to her."

Dumbo could hardly wait. He missed his mother very much.

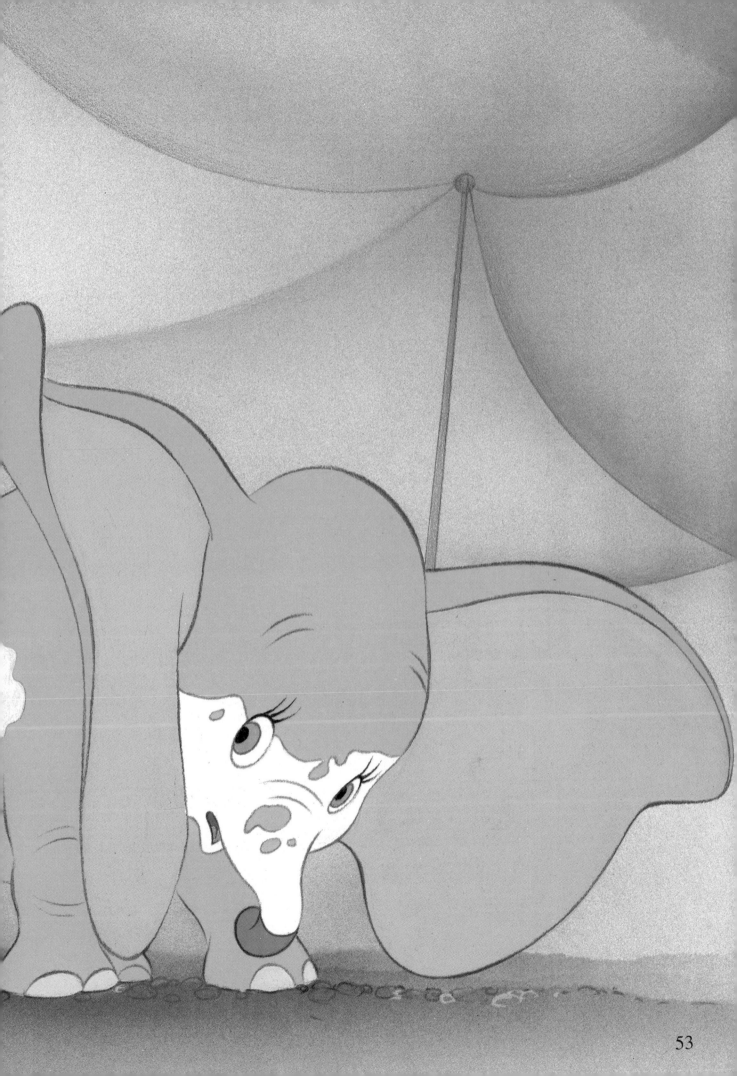

That night, as the town clocks struck midnight, Mrs. Jumbo heard a noise outside her prison car. She turned in time to see a little trunk sticking through the bars of the window.

"Dumbo, is that you?" she whispered, moving slowly toward the window. Her legs were chained to huge iron balls to keep her from moving. "Wait! I'm coming," she said, as she strained at her chains to reach the window.

Mrs. Jumbo slid her trunk between the bars and touched Dumbo. Her eyes filled with tears. "You've grown since I saw you last," she said, cradling Dumbo to her trunk. "And you smell nice and sweet. Thank goodness someone is looking after you." Rocking Dumbo gently, she began to sing a lullaby.

After some time, Timothy appeared and whispered to Dumbo that it was time to go. Dumbo and his mother sadly waved good-bye.

Dumbo's eyelids began to feel heavy and soon he was fast asleep, with strange shapes floating in his dreams. Pink and blue elephants danced and performed tricks. Dumbo had the sensation that he was flying. He could even hear birds.

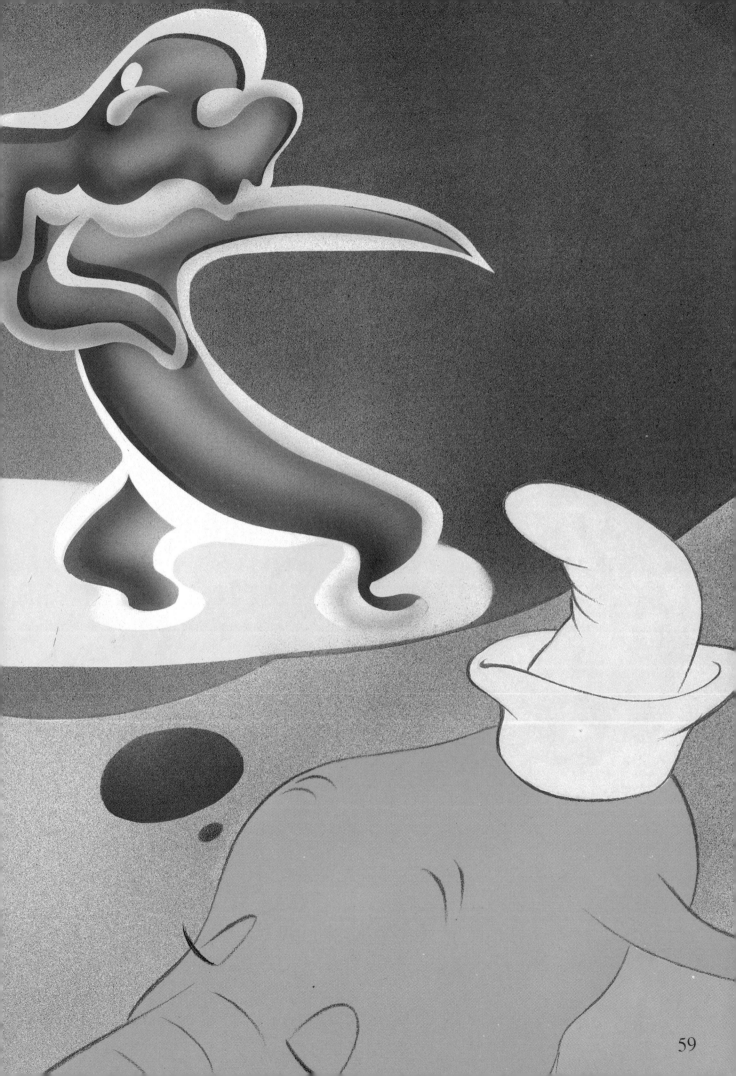

The next morning, out in the country, there was a very strange sight. High up in the crook of a tree slept a little elephant with big ears, a mouse tucked into the curve of his trunk.

A gang of crows gathered around the sleeping Dumbo and
Timothy.

"Will ya look at that giant? Never thought I'd see the day
when elephants lived in trees!" exclaimed one of the crows.

"What I want to know," said another, "is how he got up
here."

"How do you think he got here? He flew!" replied
the chief crow.

"Flew?" shouted the others. "Elephants can't fly!"

In his sleep, Dumbo heard the crows talking and thought it was a dream. He yawned sleepily and rolled over onto his side. But Dumbo wasn't dreaming, and when he rolled over, he fell out of the tree.

It was too late to grab onto the branches. Down went Dumbo, landing in a stream with an enormous splash!

Timothy tumbled out of the tree after him and landed with a tiny plop nearby.

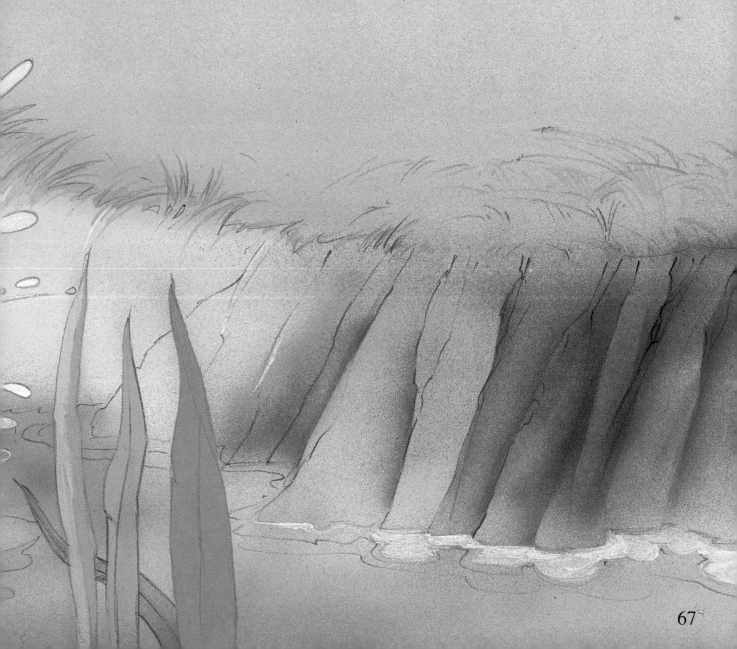

The sight of Dumbo and Timothy falling into the stream
was too much for the crows. They burst out laughing and
began to sing:

"Did you ever see an elephant fly?" sang one.

"Well, I've seen a horse fly," sang the chief.

"I've seen a peanut stand and heard a rubber band.

I've seen a needle that winked its eye.

I've seen a front porch swing and heard a diamond ring.

But I ain't never seen an elephant fly."

Timothy was not amused. "What's so funny about a poor little elephant falling out of a tree?" he demanded. Then he stopped suddenly and scratched his head. "How did you get up into the tree?" he wondered aloud.

The crows all spoke at once: "He flew."

"Flew?" Timothy cried, turning to look at Dumbo in amazement.

Dumbo blinked his eyes and stared at the crows.

"I wonder if you could do it again," mused Timothy to Dumbo. "What a circus act that would make!"

"If he did it once, he can do it again," said the chief crow. "But just to make sure," he added, handing Dumbo one of his own feathers, "I'm going to give you a magic feather."

"Now all you have to do is try," continued the crow.

"Sure, Dumbo," said Timothy. "I always said you were special. Come on. Let's give it a try."

Dumbo shook his head. He'd taken too many falls lately, and he wasn't eager to take another.

"Don't be afraid," said the crow. "All you have to do is hold on to the magic feather and jump. There's a cliff nearby where you can try."

When they reached the cliff, Dumbo took one look down and began to back away from the edge. The crows decided he needed a friendly push. Together they gave a big shove.

Dumbo closed his eyes and began to flap his ears with all his might. And instead of falling through the air, he began to float!

Timothy gave a shout of delight. "I knew you could do it! Look! We're flying!"

Dumbo opened one eye and then the other. Timothy was right. He wasn't falling; he was gliding like a bird.

Dumbo was overjoyed. This was exactly like his dream! He spread his ears out like wings and turned his body to go right or left, up or down. Before long, he was diving and swooping over houses and trees. Flying was wonderful.

Timothy began chattering away. "Just wait until the others see you! Oh, Dumbo, I just knew you'd be famous someday. But we mustn't let the others know just yet. Wait until tonight—then we'll surprise them."

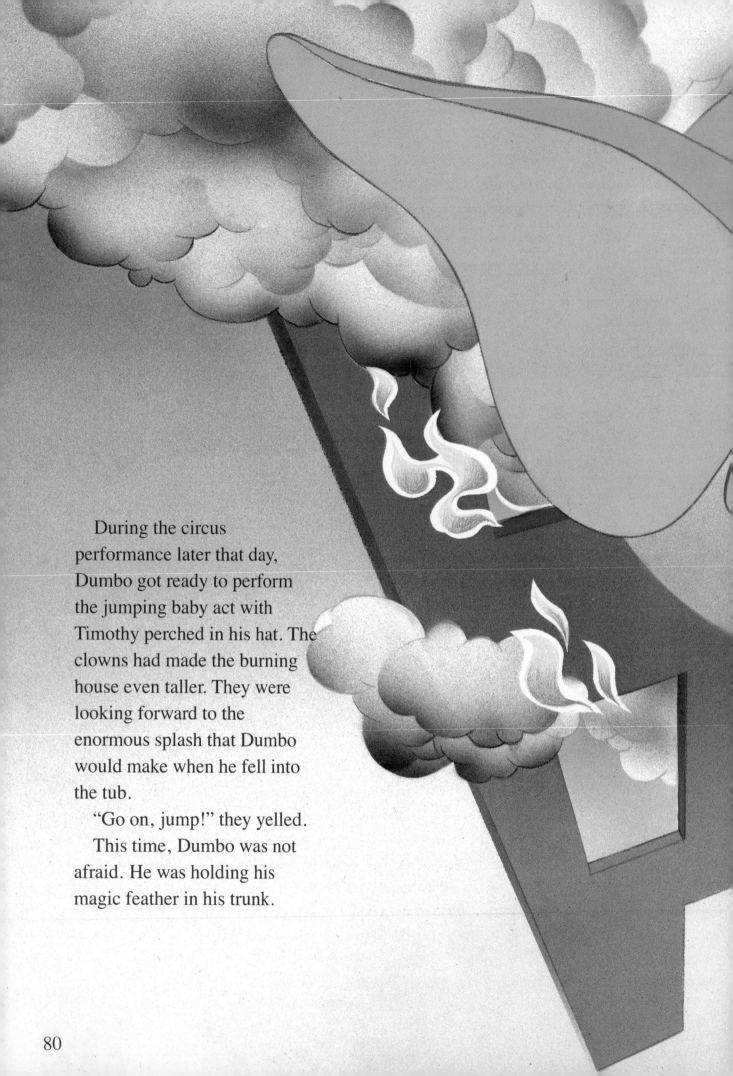

During the circus performance later that day, Dumbo got ready to perform the jumping baby act with Timothy perched in his hat. The clowns had made the burning house even taller. They were looking forward to the enormous splash that Dumbo would make when he fell into the tub.

"Go on, jump!" they yelled.

This time, Dumbo was not afraid. He was holding his magic feather in his trunk.

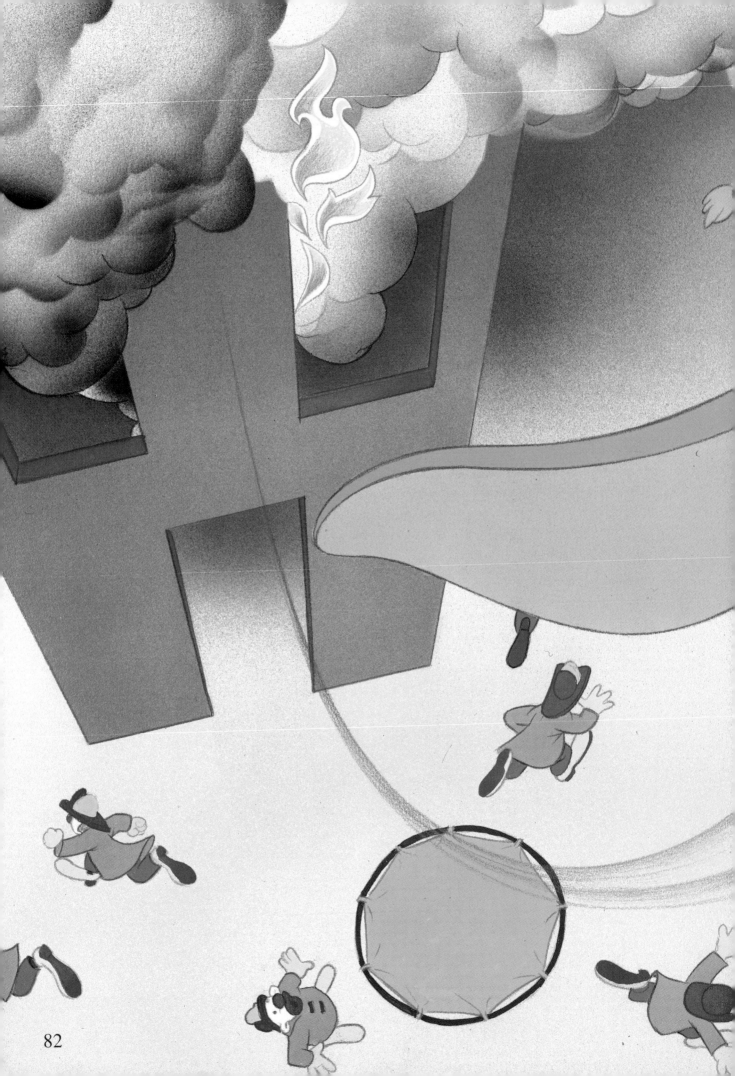

Dumbo jumped into the air, but in his excitement he dropped the feather. Frozen with fear, he began to fall, but Timothy shouted, "That feather isn't magic! You don't need it to fly, Dumbo! You can fly all by yourself!"

With that, Dumbo spread his ears. As he came within a few feet of the safety net, he changed direction. Instead of plunging into the water, he soared up toward the top of the tent.

The audience was silent.
They watched in wonder as
Dumbo soared overhead,
around and around the Big Top.

"Whee! We did it!" cried
Timothy, looking down from
his place in Dumbo's hat.

The audience began to
applaud. Then they started to
cheer. No one had ever seen
anything like it before.

"Let's show 'em a power
dive!" shouted Timothy.

Dumbo decided to have some fun. He zoomed over the heads of the clowns, and then over the ringmaster's head. The audience roared with laughter, but this time they were laughing at the clowns and not Dumbo. The terrified ringmaster jumped headfirst into the tub of water meant for Dumbo.

Thunderous applause rang in Dumbo's ears. The audience loved him. He was a star.

Dumbo became an overnight sensation. Every newspaper in the land carried his picture on the front page.

The Sun showed him power-diving in the circus tent. *The News* showed him flying over the countryside in an aviator's cap, setting a new altitude record. Everyone knew about Dumbo, the flying elephant.

Dumbo drew record crowds
in every town and village the
circus passed through. The
ringmaster was so happy with
his new star that he ordered
Dumbo's mother to be released.

Every morning, high above the circus tents, a small figure could be seen soaring across the sky. It was Dumbo, practicing his act. With Timothy in his cap, he performed nose dives, spirals, loop-the-loops, spins, rolls and landings, while his mother watched proudly from the ground.

Below, the other elephants looked on with pride. They had changed their minds about "the little runt."

"He's going to go far, that little one," said one.

"I always said he was special," said another.

"No, I was the first to say so," argued a third.

WHOO! WHOO! Chugga-Chugga-Chugga!" tooted Casey Junior as he raced down the track. He was proud of his famous passenger—Dumbo the Flying Elephant.

Published by
Penguin Books USA, Inc.
375 Hudson Street
New York, New York 10014

Produced by
Twin Books
15 Sherwood Place
Greenwich, CT 06830
USA

ISBN 0-453-03007-6

Printed in Hong Kong

4 5 6 7 8 9 10